Noah's Secret

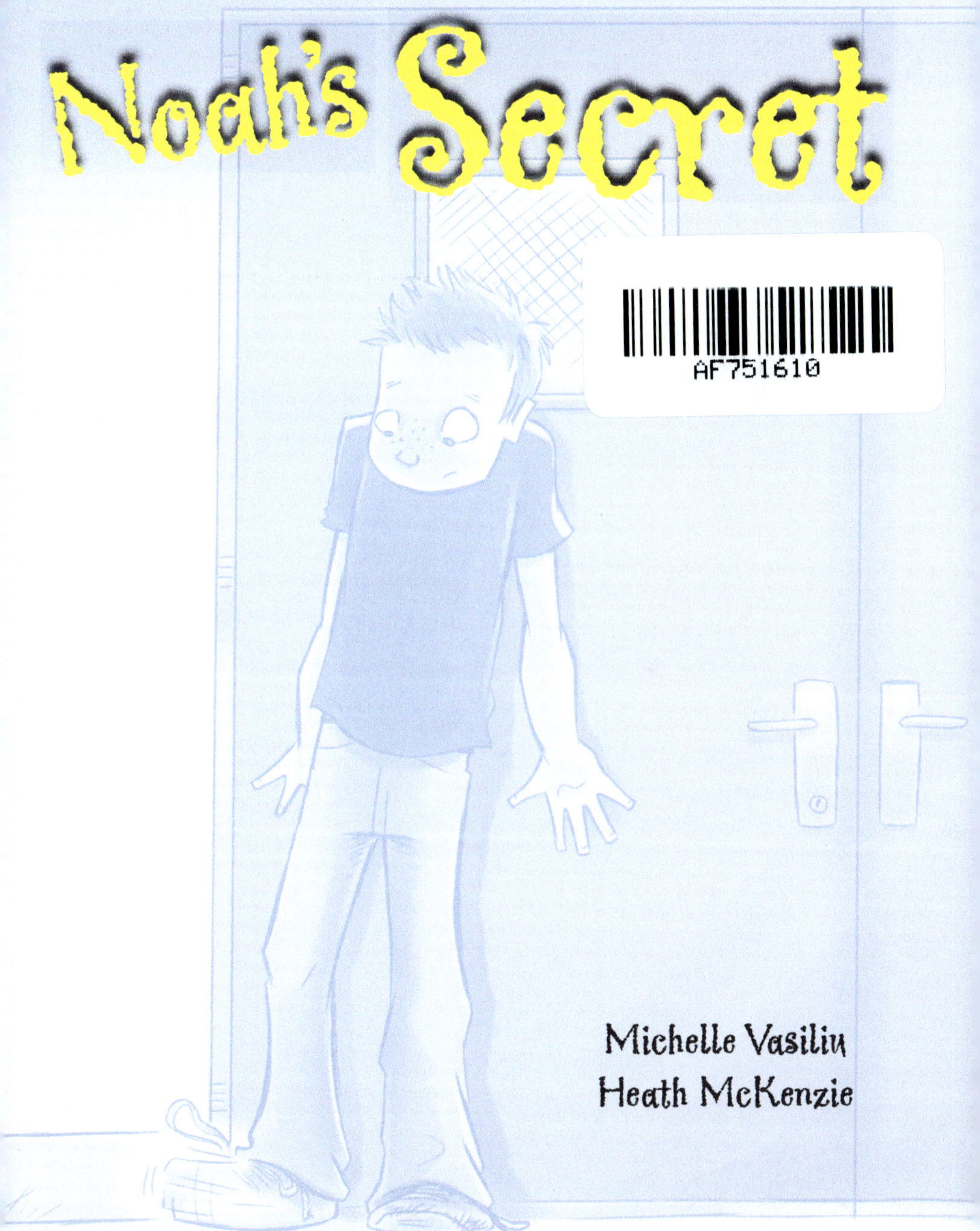

Michelle Vasiliu
Heath McKenzie

NELSON
CENGAGE Learning™

Australia • Brazil • Japan • Korea • Mexico • Singapore • Spain • United Kingdom • United States

NELSON
CENGAGE Learning™

Noah's Secret

Text: Michelle Vasiliu Illustrations: Heath McKenzie Editor: Vanessa Pellatt
Design: James Lowe
Series design: James Lowe
Production controller: Lisa Porter
Reprint: Siew Han Ong

Fast Forward Independent Texts Level 23

ISBN 978 0 17 018005 4
ISBN 978 0 17 017899 0 (set)

Cengage Learning Australia
Level 7, 80 Dorcas Street
South Melbourne, Victoria Australia 3205
Phone: 1300 790 853

Cengage Learning New Zealand
Unit 4B Rosedale Office Park
331 Rosedale Road, Albany, North Shore NZ 0632
Phone: 0508 635 766

For learning solutions, visit **cengage.com.au**

Printed in Australia by Ligare Pty Ltd
2 3 4 5 6 7 22 21 20 19

Noah's Secret

Michelle Vasiliu Heath McKenzie

Contents

CHAPTER 1

Old Friends

"Hey, Noah!
Want to play footy?"

My best friend Eddy was holding his favourite football. It was the one his dad had given him on his tenth birthday, nearly three years ago. It was covered in signatures.

Eddy dropped the ball and kicked it straight to me.

I caught it.

"Sorry, Eddy. I have to be somewhere."
I could feel my cheeks getting hot.
"Maybe tomorrow."

Eddy looked like he wanted to say something.
I quickly pushed the ball into his hands,
grabbed my school bag and ran off.
If I didn't get a move on,
I was going to be late!

CHAPTER 2

Secrets

I stood outside a closed door, listening.
"One, two, three.
One, two, three."

I heard feet moving and music playing.
The music was a bit like the stuff
my grandpa plays – old style.

"Maybe this wasn't such a good idea
after all," I thought.
It wasn't too late to turn around
and head back home.

But then I looked down at my foot.
It was tapping to the music.

I took a deep breath,
turned the door handle and entered the room.

The next day, Eddy caught up with me.

"How about that game of footy
after school?" he asked.

"Sure," I said.
"Only ... I can't."

"Need to be somewhere?" Eddy sounded hurt.

"Sort of.
Hey, maybe we could go to the movies
on Saturday," I said.
"After I buy myself some new shoes."

We both looked down at my dirty, old shoes.

"Sure!" Eddy said.
"I'll help you."

I didn't think that was such a good idea.
What if he discovered my secret?

"Let's meet up *after* I buy the shoes,"
I suggested.

"Whatever," Eddy muttered as he walked away.

CHAPTER 3

New Friends

I was still in the shop,
trying on my new shoes,
when I saw Eddy.
He was with Pete.
Pete was the captain
of the under-fifteens football team.

Pete was holding Eddy's football.

"Hi," I said when they came in.
"Going somewhere?"

"Just having a kick in the park," Eddy said.

"And I'm giving Eddy some tips," Pete added.

"Nice shoes," Eddy pointed.

Everyone looked down at my shoes.
They were shiny and new.

"Noah," a voice called.

We all turned.

It was Carmen.
She'd laughed when I'd stepped on her shoes in my first class.
Carmen said everyone did that at the start.

"Hi," she said as she walked over.

"Hi," I muttered back.

Pete cleared his throat.
"I'm Pete," he said.

"Hi Pete," Carmen smiled.

Eddy waited for me to introduce him.
But I couldn't explain how I knew Carmen.

"And this is Eddy," Pete finally said.

"Nice to meet you Eddy," Carmen replied.

"Well, we'd better get to the park
if we want to get any practice in," Eddy said.

"What about the movies?" I asked.

"I changed my mind," he replied.

I was surprised.
Didn't Eddy want to include me anymore?

"See you at school," Eddy said.

Pete looked back at Carmen
as the boys left the shop.

"Hey!" Carmen called out.
"I'll come too.
I like footy."
She turned to me and said,
"I'll catch you Monday night.
And I'll watch out for those new shoes!"

Then she ran off after Eddy and Pete.

CHAPTER 4

Time to Come Clean

I didn't hear from Eddy
for the rest of the weekend.
I wanted to tell him my secret!
After all, he was my best friend.
He'd understand
once I explained it all to him.

I tried to phone him twice,
but then I changed my mind
at the last minute.

When I got to school on Monday,
I rushed towards the footy ground.

I could see Eddy in the distance,
with a group of older kids gathered
around him.

One of the kids looked familiar.
As he turned his head slightly,
I saw that it was Pete.

It seemed like Eddy had a new best friend.

I turned around and made my way to class.

There was no sign of Eddy after school.

I wondered what Carmen had told him.
I decided to ask her that night.

Then I'd head to Eddy's and explain that I still wanted to kick the footy around with him.
And be mates.

But I also wanted to do other things.
Not just play footy.

CHAPTER 5

Dance Friends

I looked up at the sign on the front of the building – *The Paletano Dance School*.

I wondered if Carmen had arrived yet.

As I walked towards the door,
my new shoes felt tight.

"No stomping on girls' feet," I ordered myself as I opened the door.

I walked in.
A group of kids were talking together.
Some of the others were already moving
around the dance floor,
while Mrs Paletano sorted through
her paperwork.

I wanted to join in.
But I needed to talk to Carmen first.

I looked around the room and saw her
standing by the old piano.
She was talking to two kids
I couldn't quite see.

I made my way over to the piano.

"Hey, Noah."
It was Pete – with Eddy!
I couldn't help staring.

"Hi," Carmen said when she saw me.
"I asked Pete along."

Pete nodded in Eddy's direction.
"Yeah, and I reckon there's safety in numbers," Pete said.

Eddy stood up and leaned against
the piano, grinning.
"I said I'd come after Carmen
let your little secret slip," he told me.

"Sorry," Carmen shrugged.
"I thought they knew."

"Eddy, I was planning to tell you," I said.

"It's okay," he replied.
"I can understand why you'd want
to keep it a secret."

Then Eddy pointed at Carmen and Pete.

Carmen was showing Pete the steps.
She was smiling.

"I know that some guys might not want to learn to dance," Eddy said.
"But I think this could be a lot of fun!"
He looked over at a group of girls.

"And football's not the only thing I'm interested in," Eddy continued.

"That makes two of us!" Pete added, as he and Carmen joined us. "And you never know – these steps might help with our football skills," Pete smiled.

"And Pete's fitness!" Eddy whispered.

"Maybe," I laughed.

Then Eddy nodded towards his shoes
and we all looked down.
They were shiny and new,
just like mine.

I elbowed Eddy and smiled.
He elbowed me back.
We all laughed.

"Right everyone!
Let's get started," called Mrs Paletano.